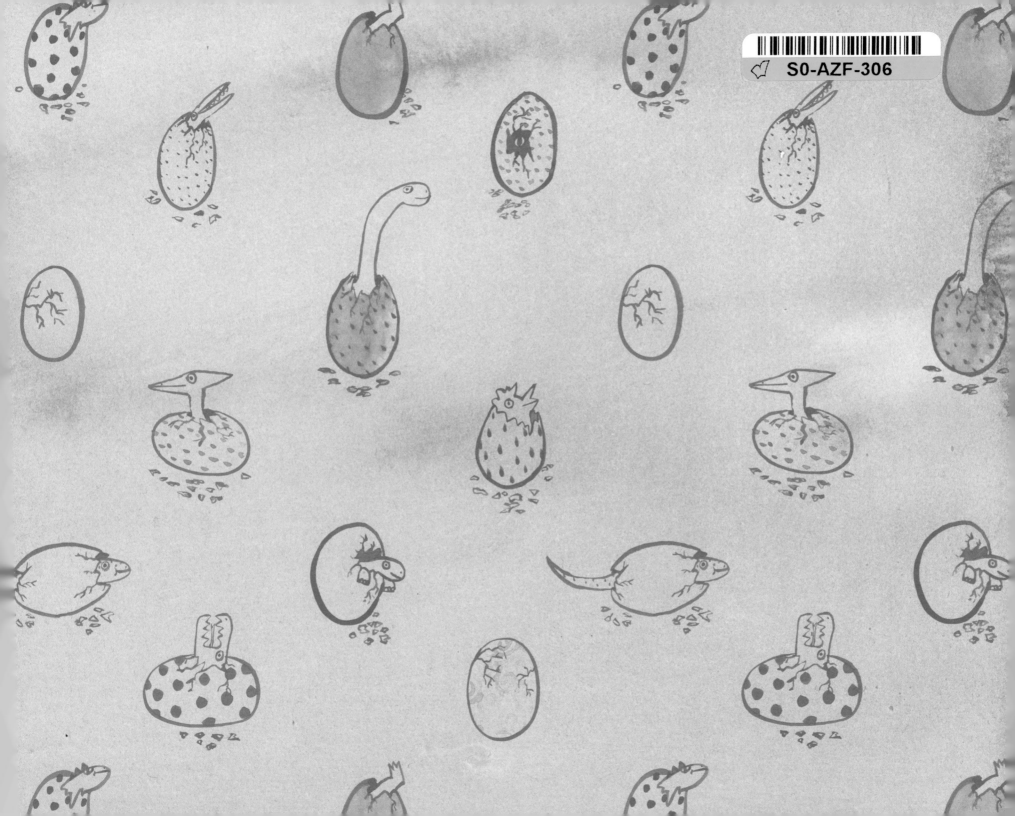

For Poojan, Emily, Ethan & Evan. RAWR!
—J. W.

For Jack. Thank you. I couldn't have done this without your hugs,
shoulder rubs, and laughter, not to mention your brilliant color
sense and drawing advice. I absolutely adore you.
—H. B.

SIMON & SCHUSTER BOOKS FOR YOUNG READERS
An imprint of Simon & Schuster Children's Publishing Division
1230 Avenue of the Americas, New York, New York 10020
Text © 2022 by Jennifer Wagh • Illustration © 2022 by Hallie Bateman
Book design by Lizzy Bromley © 2022 by Simon & Schuster, Inc.
All rights reserved, including the right of reproduction in whole or in part in any form.
SIMON & SCHUSTER BOOKS FOR YOUNG READERS and related marks are trademarks of Simon & Schuster, Inc.
For information about special discounts for bulk purchases, please contact
Simon & Schuster Special Sales at 1-866-506-1949 or business@simonandschuster.com.
The Simon & Schuster Speakers Bureau can bring authors to your live event. For more information or to book an event, contact the
Simon & Schuster Speakers Bureau at 1-866-248-3049 or visit our website at www.simonspeakers.com.
The text for this book was set in Brandon Grotesque and Post Box.
The illustrations for this book were rendered in ink, watercolor, gouache, crayon, and colored pencil.
Manufactured in China • 0122 SCP • First Edition
2 4 6 8 10 9 7 5 3 1
Library of Congress Cataloging-in-Publication Data
Names: Wagh, Jennifer, author. | Bateman, Hallie, illustrator.
Title: Eggasaurus / Jennifer Wagh ; illustrated by Hallie Bateman.
Description: First edition. | New York : Simon & Schuster Books for Young Readers, [2022] |
Audience: Ages 4–8. | Audience: Grades K–1. |
Summary: In this story told entirely in letters, Maximus orders a dinosaur egg through the mail, and every time
he tries to send it back or refuse additional offers from Eggasaurus, Inc., he is in more trouble.
Identifiers: LCCN 2021009860 (print) | LCCN 2021009861 (ebook) |
ISBN 9781534450066 (hardcover) | ISBN 9781534450073 (ebook)
Subjects: LCSH: Dinosaurs—Juvenile fiction. | Fathers and sons—Juvenile fiction. | Letters—Juvenile fiction. | Humorous stories. | CYAC: Dinosaurs as
pets—Fiction. | Eggs—Fiction. | Fathers and sons—Fiction. | Letters—Fiction. | Humorous stories. | LCGFT: Humorous fiction. | Epistolary fiction.
Classification: LCC PZ7.1.W33 Egg 2022 (print) | LCC PZ7.1.W33 (ebook) | DDC [E]—dc23
LC record available at https://lccn.loc.gov/2021009860
LC ebook record available at https://lccn.loc.gov/2021009861

EGGASAURUS

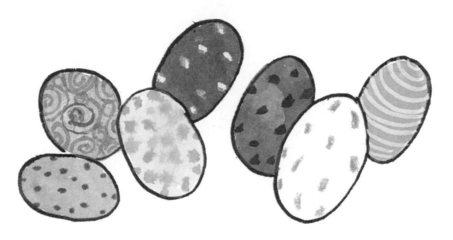

Written by Jennifer Wagh
Illustrated by Hallie Bateman

Simon & Schuster Books for Young Readers
New York London Toronto Sydney New Delhi

Dear Customer,
Thank you for your
Eggasaurus purchase.

Your eggs may contain herbivore,
omnivore, or carnivore.
Please keep eggs warm and rotated.
Have a variety of foods available.
They enjoy listening to music.
NO REFUNDS!
Thank you for your purchase,
Eggasaurus, Inc.

P.S. I am keeping the eggs warm with my fuzziest sweater.

Dear Customer,
We are sorry your father
is unhappy with your
Eggasaurus product.
But as previously stated
there are NO REFUNDS.
Please accept these
two additional eggs as
compensation.

Thank you,
Eggasaurus, Inc.

Dear Customer,
We are sending an additional assortment of eggs for your gratitude.
Thank you,
Eggasaurus, Inc.

P.S. Please note: rock 'n' roll gets them hatching.

Dear Eggasaurus, Inc.,
Dad was floored after the last delivery.
Maximus

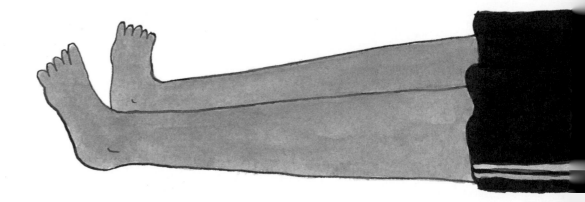

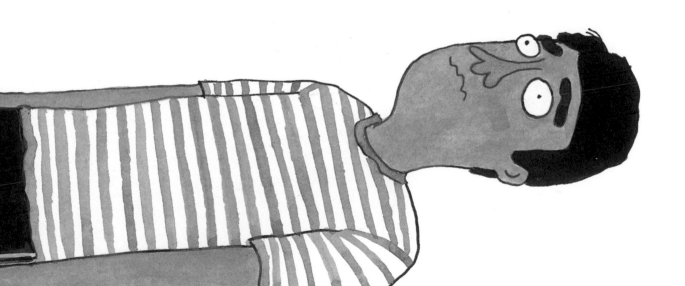

Dear Customer,
We are delighted your father was
overwhelmed with joy.
Tell your friends and family about
our five-star service.
We have included gift certificates
for you to use or pass along.
Thank you,
Eggasaurus, Inc.

Dear Eggasaurus, Inc.,
I will definitely tell my
friends about Eggasaurus, Inc.
My dad will too!

Maximus

Dear Eggasaurus, Inc.,
They went crazy for the ball and Frisbees.
There are dinosaurs all over our garden!
Maximus

Dear Customer,
Young dinosaurs love
the outdoors!

We recommend three
hours of fresh air and
exercise daily.

Thank you,
Eggasaurus, Inc.

Dear Eggasaurus, Inc.,
Dad said we are an all-out dinosaur day care.

Maximus

Dear Customer,
We are intrigued by your proposal of becoming an official Dinosaur Day Care. We are sending you an authentic certificate with a special delivery.

Thank you,
Eggasaurus, Inc.

Eggasaurus, Inc.

OFFICIAL ★ CERTIFICATE

Loyal Eggasaurus customers, we are pleased to announce Maximus's Dinosaur Day Care Service

OFFICIALLY OFFICIAL